To Abigail

THE LITTLEST REINDEER

A SILVER STAR BOOK

By Johanna DeWitt

Pictures by Phoebe Erickson

CHILDRENS PRESS, CHICAGO

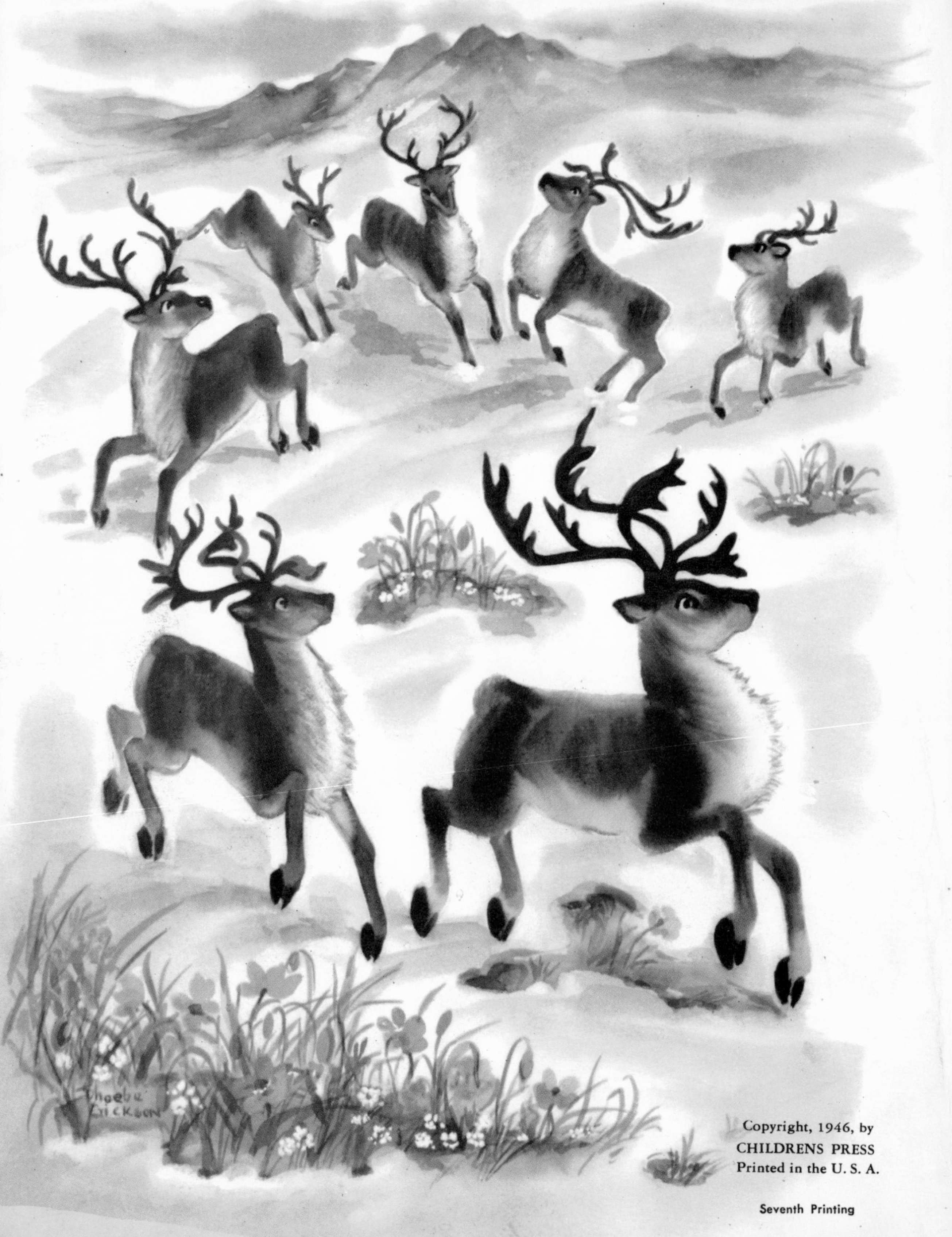

Seventh Printing

The littlest reindeer was unhappy. Flowers were blooming through the arctic snow. Birds were singing. All the other reindeer were prancing up and down, waving their antlers and making merry. Only the littlest reindeer stood alone and felt sad. He was ashamed to prance with the others because he had no antlers.

The biggest reindeer had antlers six feet high and six feet wide. The next biggest reindeer had antlers five feet high and five feet wide. Even the next to the littlest reindeer had antlers that were half a foot high and half a foot wide. Only the littlest reindeer had none at all. He stood alone and was ashamed.

The biggest reindeer called to him. "Come join the dance, little one. It is our last dance near the arctic circle this year."

But the littlest reindeer shook his head and stayed where he was.

The next day the biggest reindeer called all the reindeer to him. "Come with me," he said in a loud voice. "Winter is coming. To-day we go south to the land of the woods so we may eat when the snow is deep. Come!" he said and tossed his antlers.

All the reindeer lined up in single file behind the biggest reindeer and followed him. All but the littlest reindeer. He hid behind a large rock and cried and cried as he watched the others march away.

The air grew colder and the flowers stopped blooming. A snowbird lighted on a rock by the littlest reindeer and cocked his head in wonder.

"What's the matter here?" asked the snowbird. "Why didn't you go with the others, little reindeer?"

"I was ashamed to go because I have no antlers," cried the littlest reindeer.

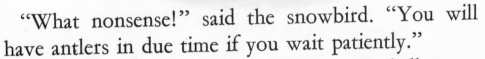

"What nonsense!" said the snowbird. "You will have antlers in due time if you wait patiently."

"Not I," said the littlest reindeer. "I shall never have antlers."

"Go join the others and wait for spring," said the snowbird. "See then if you have antlers."

The littlest reindeer said nothing. The snowbird snapped his bill twice in disgust and shrugged. "All right, then," he said, and flew away.

Snow began to fall. First slowly and then faster and faster. But the littlest reindeer did not notice. Neither did he notice a great musk ox coming slowly from the north. But the musk ox saw the littlest reindeer and stopped beside him.

"What's the matter here?" rumbled the musk ox in a large voice. "Why didn't you go with the others, little reindeer?"

"I was ashamed to go because I have no antlers," cried the littlest reindeer.

"What nonsense!" roared the musk ox.

"You can say nonsense," said the littlest reindeer. "You *have* horns. You can walk with your kind and not be ashamed." The littlest reindeer looked up through his tears at the musk ox's horns curving down in two great curves.

"You will have antlers in due time if you wait patiently," said the musk ox. "Go join the others and wait for spring."

"Not I," said the littlest reindeer. "I shall never have antlers."

The musk ox snorted twice in disgust and walked off through the snow.

It grew colder and colder. The littlest reindeer cried and cried. All of a sudden one of his tears froze into a shining bead of ice. Very soon a long glittering chain of frozen tears hung from the littlest reindeer's eyes. He could cry no more.

"I must cry because I have no antlers," said the littlest reindeer. He snapped off his icicle tears and ran across the snow. "Perhaps if I go toward the south my tears will not freeze," he said. So he tried to go the same way the other reindeer had gone.

Night-time came, and the littlest reindeer wondered if he would ever reach the south. Just then he took one step and there was no snow. His little hooves struck something hard and slippery.

"Am I south now?" he wondered. "I shall see if I can cry. But as soon as he squeezed out one tear it froze in the corner of his eye. He stamped his foot in anger, and at that moment the northern lights filled the sky with a thousand ribbons of light. The littlest reindeer saw that he was on a ledge of ice at the edge of the sea. Right beside him a sleepy walrus lifted his head.

"What's the matter here?" barked the walrus. "Why do you stamp your foot and wake me up?"

"I am angry because I cannot cry." said the littlest reindeer.

"And why must you cry?" asked the walrus.

"Because I have no antlers," said the littlest reindeer.

"What nonsense!" said the walrus.

"You can say nonsense," said the littlest reindeer. "You have tusks. You can swim with your kind and not be afraid." The littlest reindeer could see the walrus's great white tusks shining in the gleam of the northern lights.

"Now you think I have always had tusks?" asked the walrus. "No. I had to wait for them to grow. You must wait for antlers to grow. When it is time for you to have them, you will have them."

"Not I," said the littlest reindeer. "I shall never have antlers."

At that moment a great white shape moved out from behind a hill of ice. It was a polar bear and his eyes shone red in the northern lights.

Phoebe
Erickson

The littlest reindeer did not see him. He was saying
to the walrus, "Just tell me which way is south so
I can go there and cry. I must cry because I have
no antlers."

The walrus snorted twice in disgust, turned from
the ledge of ice, and splashed into the sea.

Then the littlest reindeer saw the polar bear.

"I like little reindeer that have no antlers," said the
polar bear. "They are very tender eating indeed."

The littlest reindeer was so frightened that for a minute he could not move. The polar bear came nearer and nearer, padding on his great white paws.

The littlest reindeer picked up his hooves and ran. The polar bear ran after him.

"Don't be ashamed of not having antlers," called the polar bear. "I don't mind a bit."

Suddenly the northern lights went out. The ribbons of light were gone from the sky and the littlest reindeer was running in the dark.

"Ho, little reindeer!" called the polar bear. "Don't run off into the dark so I can't find you."

The littlest reindeer did not listen to the polar bear. He ran on and on into the dark. He ran until he could no longer hear the polar bear calling to him. He ran until the dark was gone and the sun peeked over the horizon.

The littlest reindeer ran faster. He did not know if he was running north or south. He knew only that he must run faster than the polar bear, who was getting closer and closer.

Then the littlest reindeer knew that he had been running south all night. He was in the land of the woods. There was no snow here. Instead the ground was covered with thick brown moss.

"Now I can cry," said the littlest reindeer. And so he did.

"What's the matter here?" asked a moose. "Why are you not with the other reindeer?"

"I am ashamed because I have no antlers," said the littlest reindeer.

"What nonsense!" said the moose.

"You have antlers," said the littlest reindeer. "You can run with your kind and not be ashamed."

"So you think I have always had antlers?" asked the moose. "No. I had to wait for them to grow. You must wait for them to grow. When it is time for you to have them, you will have them."

"Not I," said the littlest reindeer. "I shall never have antlers."

The moose snorted in disgust and went off through the woods. The littlest reindeer was all alone.

He looked around the quiet woods. He looked at the ground that was covered with thick brown moss. "Here I can rest and eat and cry," he said. And so he did, day after day, for a long time.

One morning his head began to itch. He rubbed his head against the rough bark of a tree and thought no more about it. Every day his head itched and, oddly enough, it itched right where his antlers should have been.

Then one day the littlest reindeer sniffed the air and knew that something was different. The sun crept up and up the sky until it poured sunshine down through the trees. Leaves popped out and birds began to sing. The littlest reindeer thought about the cool stretches of snow in the north. He thought of the biggest reindeer with his antlers six feet high and six feet wide.

Suddenly there was a thundering sound in the distance. It came closer and closer. The littlest reindeer peeked out from behind a tree and at that moment the whole herd of reindeer rushed past him, heading north. The biggest reindeer was leading and he was waving his antlers. The others were pounding after him.

When they were out of sight the littlest reindeer crept out from behind the tree.

"Spring!" he said. "All the other reindeer are going north to dance up and down the arctic snow. All but me."

"Why not you?" asked a voice from somewhere.

The littlest reindeer was surprised. "Who's there?" he asked.

"It is I, the snowbird," said the voice.

"Where are you?" asked the littlest reindeer. The snowbird's voice seemed to come from above, but when the littlest reindeer looked up he could not see him.

"Look down," said the snowbird. "Look down into that pool of water beside you and see what you see."

The littlest reindeer went nearer to the pool and looked into the clear water. Then he gulped and looked again.

He saw the snowbird perched on the top of his own, his very own, foot-long antlers.

"Antlers " shouted the littlest reindeer. "I have antlers!"

"Very fine antlers, too," said the snowbird.

"It was the antlers growing that made my head itch," said the littlest reindeer.

"Of course," said the snowbird. "But you wouldn't believe that sometimes you have to wait for something worth having." The snowbird snapped his bill shut and flew to a tree.

"Think of the tears you have wasted!" shouted the snowbird.

But the littlest reindeer did not hear him. He was running as fast as he could to join the other reindeer in the first dance of the year across the arctic snow.

4966